I Am a Wish

Archway Publishing books may be ordered through booksellers or by contacting:

Archway Publishing
1663 Liberty Drive
Bloomington, IN 47403
www.archwaypublishing.com
1-(888)-242-5904

ISBN: 978-1-4808-0090-8 (hc)
ISBN: 978-1-4808-0094-6 (sc)
ISBN: 978-1-4808-0089-2 (e)

Printed in the United States of America

Archway Publishing rev. date: 5/30/2013

I Am a Wish

The Incredibly True Story of the Dandelion

RERE THE STORYTELLER

Give me your curious, your whimsical, your dreamers of dreams yearning to breathe life into every seam. Those few who color outside the pages, you know those little sages: to them I send these wishes and hopes, near and far. For them, I lift my wand to the stars in the magic of who they are.

—*ReRe the Storyteller*

It was on a very ordinary day
In a very ordinary place,

In a place where swings would fly
And slides climbed all the way up
to the sky.

Behind this place, there lived
a field of sunflowers.

They would soak in sun
and have fun for hours.

On this same field, there was this thing that stuck out right in the middle.

And truth be told, it was rather little.

All the sunflowers talked and pointed at this strange looking thing.

Not a single one of them could see the joy it would bring.

This thing didn't have pretty petals like all the rest.

It was a lesser flower, and that was at best.

It had this fuzz that would whirl in the wind.

It floated …

It spun …

It got in the way of
the big bright sun.

Rumor had it this thing they called
a dandelion was actually a weed.

Its hair, well ... each one was its
very own seed.

It just wasn't like anything they
had ever seen.

Then a very curious sunflower asked,
"What does any of this mean?"

The dandelion turned and said, "I am a *wish*, and that *wish* is me. I am what you want to see."

None of the sunflowers understood or
knew what a *wish* was

                                Or what it does.

They had begun to wonder if it was a name,
So then this dandelion began to explain.

A *wish* is a desire.

It's a hope.

It's a dream.

It's a truth fulfilled.

The heart keeps these *wishes*
as secrets locked away,

That is, until it is ready
for that special day.

"When a child or
grownup sees me,

They think of all the things

they *wish* to be.

They pluck me right from
the ground.

And then whisper softly, so you

cannot hear a sound.

They whisper their secret
throughout all my hair

As they tell me what their
hearts hold dear.

Each word they silently blow,
It makes my hair begin to snow

As I float and scatter all about
So full of hope and not a single doubt.

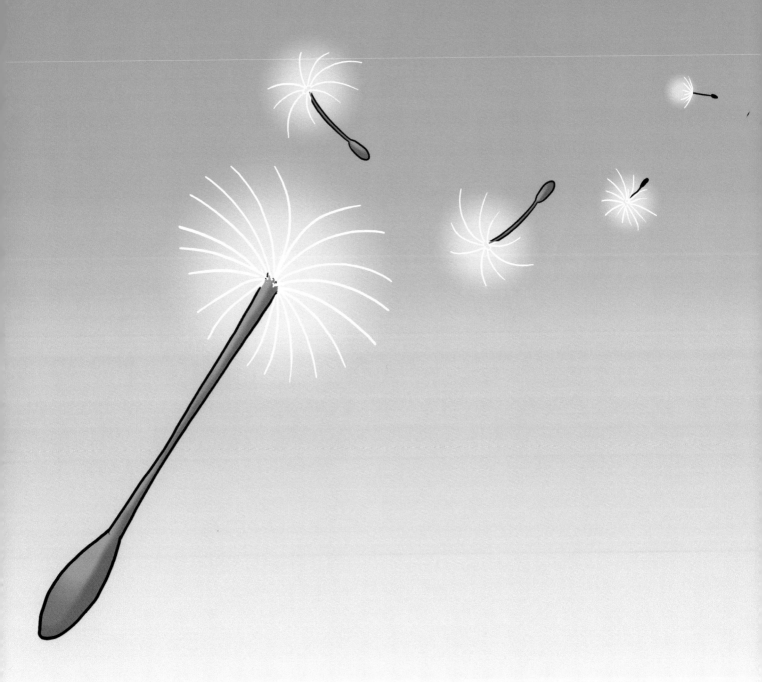

I carry this very *wish* to everything.

I whisper it throughout the sky.

I carry it across the ocean.

I reach it on high.

It is then carried far and wide.

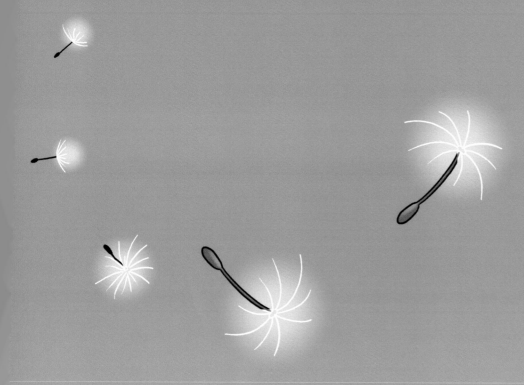

I whisper it to all the trees.
Then they tell it to each small breeze.
I take their *wish* all around
Until the day I gently let it in the ground.

I am planted into the seeds that grow,
And what happens from there is a
spectacular magical show:

Every plant,

Every creature,

And every seed

Makes this *wish* come true.

And now I will tell you
something you never knew:

The magic in a *wish* is not held within me.
It is the *wisher* who makes it come to be.

The *wisher's* belief is the
magical power in who I am.

        For I am simply just a *wish;*
        this is what you see

As I await a *wisher* to tell me
who that shall be."

At that moment a little girl ran up and plucked the dandelion from the ground.

All the sunflowers watched and didn't make a single sound.

She held it way up into the sky and closed her eyes really tight.
Then she waited until she felt it was quite right.

She pulled the dandelion close to her lips,
softly whispered, and let go of her *wish*.

The sunflowers watched the hairs scatter
all about and Looked at this little girl, full of
hope and not a single doubt.

This little girl made a *wish* of her own
On the only dandelion the
sunflowers had ever known.

What happened from there,
Well, that dandelion already did share.

But in case you needed
one last clue,

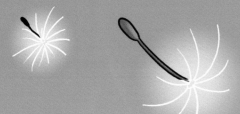

That little girl's *wish* …
Well, it just came true.

CPSIA information can be obtained
at www.ICGtesting.com
Printed in the USA
LVIC04n1259131215
466476LV00013B/50